Merry Christ
to
Avi from
Grandma Myra

CHRISTMAS C·A·R·O·L

I dedicate this edition of *A Christmas Carol*
to my mother and father,
Barbara and Walter R. Sturrock,
for all the love and support
they gave my art career.

Walt Sturrock

ILLUSTRATOR'S NOTE

I have always loved the story of *A Christmas Carol* and the character of Ebenezer Scrooge. Being a hopeful person, there is nothing nicer than illustrating such a happy story. The author, Charles Dickens, created a man with an icy-cold heart, and it was an enjoyable challenge to paint Scrooge as his heart finally melted and glowed with warmth.

I believe that this is truly the most classic Christmas story. No other book captures so many feelings in such a wonderful way. Every age can enjoy Mr. Dickens' timeless Christmas message of the joy of giving.

When I began planning the paintings for this book, I was worried about creating new images. After re-reading the story several times, it was easy for me to create the characters as I saw them. Using full pages for the pictures is my favorite way to illustrate a story, and illustrating my favorite Christmas story was very special to me. I hope that you enjoy reading this book as much as I enjoyed illustrating it.

A CHRISTMAS C·A·R·O·L

By CHARLES DICKENS

Illustrated By
WALT STURROCK

The Unicorn Publishing House
New Jersey

Designed by Jean L. Scrocco
Edited by Michael Wendt
Printed in Singapore by Toppan Printing Co.
Pte. Ltd. through Palace Press, San Francisco, CA.
Typography by Multifacit Graphics, Keyport, NJ
Reproduction Photography by the Color Wheel, NY, NY

For information, contact Jean L. Scrocco at
The Unicorn Publishing House, Inc.,
120 American Rd., Morris Plains, NJ 07950

Distributed to the book trade in Canada
by Doubleday Canada, Toronto, ON

Distributed to the gift and toy trade in Canada
by Brigetta Import, Inc., Concord, ON

Printing History 15 14 13 12 11 10 9 8 7 6 5 4 3 2

Library of Congress Cataloging-in-Publication Data
Dickens, Charles, 1812-1870.
A Christmas carol / by Charles Dickens ; illustrated by Walt Sturrock.
p. 80 cm.
Summary: Through the intervention of four ghosts,
Ebenezer Scrooge is shown the spirit of Christmas.
ISBN 0-88101-087-1 : $5.95
[1. Christmas - Fiction. 2. Ghosts - Fiction. 3. England - Fiction]
I. Sturrock, Walt, 1961 - ill. II. Title.
PZ7.D55Cew 1988
[Fic] — dc10
88-10189
CIP AC1961 - ill. II. Title.

More Colorful Classics
In This
Easy-to-Read
Little Unicorn Classic Series

PETER PAN
ANTIQUE FAIRY TALES
PINOCCHIO
THE WIZARD OF OZ
HEIDI
POLLYANNA
DAVY AND THE GOBLIN
TWENTY THOUSAND LEAGUES

CAST OF CHARACTERS

Vincent Colandrea - Ebenezer Scrooge
Gene O'Brien - Nephew; Ghost of Christmas Future
William McGuire - Jacob Marley's Ghost
Kenneth Taylor, Jr. - Ghost of Christmas Past; Ignorance
Jennifer Baldwin - Little Fan
Matthew McCann - Young Scrooge
Shirley DeVincenzi - Mrs. Fezziwig; Mrs. Dilber
Joe DeVincenzi - Mr. Fezziwig
Robert L. Rebach - Ghost of Christmas Present
Walt Sturrock - Bob Cratchit
Robbie McCann - Tiny Tim
Judy McCann - Mrs. Cratchit
Jim McCann - Master Peter Cratchit
Lisa DeVincenzi - Martha Cratchit
Cheryl DeVincenzi - Cratchit Daughter
Alicia DeVincenzi - Cratchit Daughter
Brian McGee - Cratchit Son
Jennifer Taylor - Want
Steve Krozser - Business Man
Doug Corriston - Business Man
Joseph D. Scrocco, Jr. - Old Joe
Greg Hildebrandt - Undertaker
Jean L. Scrocco - Cleaning Woman
James Holmes - Butcher
Alan Braun - Errand Boy
Heidi Corso - Nephew's Wife

LIST OF ILLUSTRATIONS

CHRISTMAS C·A·R·O·L

Marley was dead: to begin with. There is no doubt whatever about that. The burial register was signed by the clergyman, the clerk, the undertaker, and the chief mourner, Ebenezer Scrooge. Old Marley was as dead as a doornail.

Scrooge and he were business partners for I don't know how many years. Scrooge was his only friend. And even Scrooge was not so dreadfully cut up by the sad event that he wasn't an excellent man of business on the very day of the funeral.

Scrooge never painted out Marley's name on the door of "Scrooge and Marley." He answered to either name; it was all the same to him.

Oh! but he was a tight-fisted hand at the grindstone, Scrooge! a squeezing, grasping, scraping, clutching old sinner!

The weather had little influence on Scrooge. No

warmth could warm, nor wintry weather chill him. No wind blew bitterer than he, no falling snow or pelting rain was more intent upon its purpose. The cold within him froze his features, nipped his pointed nose, shrivelled his cheek, stiffened his walk; made his eyes red and his thin lips blue.

Nobody ever stopped him to say, "My dear Scrooge, how are you?" No beggars asked him for money, no man or woman ever asked directions. But what did Scrooge care? Scrooge deliberately kept away from people.

Once upon a time on Christmas Eve, old Scrooge sat busy at his desk. It was cold, bleak, biting weather. He could hear the people in the court outside, beating their hands together and stamping their feet to warm them. The city clocks had only just struck three, but it was quite dark already and thick fog came pouring in at every keyhole.

The door of Scrooge's counting-house was open that he might keep his eye on his clerk, who was copying letters in a little room beyond. Scrooge had a very small fire, but the clerk's fire was even smaller, for Scrooge kept the coal-box in his own room, miserly giving out bits of coal. The clerk put on his white comforter, and tried unsuccessfully to warm himself at the candle.

"A merry Christmas, uncle! God save you!" cried the cheerful voice of Scrooge's nephew, Fred, as he entered. His handsome face was in a glow, his eyes sparkling.

"Bah!" said Scrooge, "Humbug! Merry Christmas? What reason have you to be merry? You're poor enough."

"Come, then," returned the nephew happily. "What

reason have you to be gloomy? You're rich enough. Don't be cross, uncle."

"What else can I be," asked the uncle, "when I live in such a world of fools? What's Christmas time to you but a time for finding yourself a year older, and not an hour richer. If I could work my will, every idiot who goes about with 'Merry Christmas' on his lips, should be boiled with his own pudding, and buried with a stake of holly through his heart. No, nephew, keep Christmas in your own way, and let me keep it in mine!"

"Keep it!" repeated Fred. "But you don't keep it."

"Let me leave it alone, then," said Scrooge. "Much good may it do you! Much good it has ever done you!"

"There are many good things from which I have not made money, including Christmas," returned the nephew, "but I am sure I have always thought of Christmas time as a good time. Apart from its sacred name, it's a kind, forgiving, charitable, pleasant time — when men and women seem to open their shut-up hearts freely. Therefore, uncle, though it has never put a scrap of gold or silver in my pocket, I believe that it *has* done me good; and I say, 'God bless it!' Come eat with us tomorrow, uncle."

Scrooge said that he would see him — yes, he said it on Christmas Eve — in another world first.

"But why?" cried Fred. "Why?"

"Why did you get married?" said Scrooge.

"Because I fell in love."

"Because you fell in love!" growled Scrooge, sarcastically. "Good afternoon."

"But you never came to see me before that happened. Why give it as a reason now? I ask nothing of you; why can't we be friends?"

"Good afternoon," said Scrooge.

"I am sorry, with all my heart, to find you so determined. We have never had any quarrel. So a Merry Christmas, uncle, and a Happy New Year!"

His nephew left the room without an angry word. He stopped at the outer door to give season's greetings to the clerk, Bob Cratchit.

"There's another fellow," muttered Scrooge, "my clerk, with fifteen shillings a week, and a wife and family, talking about a Merry Christmas."

As Scrooge's nephew left, two other people entered. They were pleasant, portly gentlemen, and now stood, with hats off, in Scrooge's office.

"Have I the pleasure of addressing Mr. Scrooge or Mr. Marley?" asked one of the gentlemen, referring to his list.

"Mr. Marley died seven years ago this very night," Scrooge replied.

"No doubt his giving nature survives in his partner. At this festive season of the year, Mr. Scrooge," said the gentleman, taking up a pen, "it is more than usually desirable that we should help the poor."

"Are there no prisons?" asked Scrooge.

"Plenty of prisons," said the gentleman.

"Are the workhouses still in operation? And the Treadmill and Poor Law?"

"They are. Still," returned the gentleman, "I wish I could say they were not."

"Oh! I was afraid, from what you said at first, that

something had happened to stop them in their useful course," said Scrooge.

"A few of us are trying to raise a fund to buy the Poor some meat and drink, and means of warmth," returned the gentleman. "What shall I put you down for?"

"Nothing!" Scrooge replied. "I help to support the establishments I have mentioned and those who are badly off must go there."

"Many can't go there; many would rather die."

"If they would rather die," said Scrooge, "they had better do it, and decrease the extra population. Good afternoon, gentlemen!"

Seeing that it would be useless to continue, the gentlemen left. Scrooge returned to his work with a very good opinion of himself.

Meanwhile, the fog and darkness thickened. The cold became intense. A young boy, gnawed by the hungry cold as bones are gnawed by dogs, stooped down to carol at Scrooge's keyhole, but at the first sound Scrooge seized the ruler with such energy, that the singer fled in terror.

At length the hour of shutting up the counting-house arrived. "You'll want all day tomorrow, I suppose?" said Scrooge.

"If quite convenient, sir," replied Bob Cratchit.

"It's not convenient," said Scrooge, "and it's not fair. If I was to hold back half-a-crown for it, you'd feel yourself ill used. And yet you don't think *me* ill used, when I pay for no work."

"It is only once a year," Bob said.

"A poor excuse for picking a man's pocket every

twenty-fifth of December!" said Scrooge. "Be here all the earlier next morning!"

The clerk promised that he would and Scrooge walked out with a growl. Bob closed the office in a twinkling and, with the ends of his comforter dangling below his waist, ran home to Camden Town.

Scrooge took his gloomy dinner in his usual gloomy tavern. Then he went home to his room which was in a depressing building. One could almost imagine that when it was a young house, it had run here during a game of hide-and-seek and had forgotten the way out. It was dreary for nobody lived in it but Scrooge; the other rooms being all offices. The fog and frost hung on the gateway.

Now, it is a fact, that there was nothing at all particular about the knocker on the door, except that it was large. Also, Scrooge had not thought of Marley, since mentioning his seven-years' dead partner that afternoon. Yet Scrooge, putting his key in the lock of the door, saw not a knocker, but Marley's face.

Marley's face! It was not a black shadow as the other objects in the yard were, but had a dismal light about it. It was not angry, but looked at Scrooge as Marley used to look: with ghostly spectacles turned up upon its ghostly forehead. The hair was moving strangely, as if by breath or hot-air. Although the eyes were wide open, they were perfectly motionless.

As Scrooge stared at the face, it became a knocker again.

To say that he was not startled would be untrue. But he put his hand upon the key he had dropped, turned it sturdily, walked in and lighted his candle. Before he shut

the door, however, he *did* look cautiously behind it first, but there was nothing so he said "Pooh, pooh!" and closed it with a bang. After locking the door, Scrooge walked across the hall, and slowly up the dark stairs picking extra bits of wax from the candle as he went. Darkness is cheap and Scrooge liked it.

Recalling the face, he walked through his rooms to see that all was right. Quite satisfied, he closed his door, and double-locked himself in, which was not his custom. He put on his dressing-gown, slippers, and nightcap; and sat down before the fire to have his gruel.

As he threw his head back in the chair, his glance happened to rest upon a bell that hung in the room. It was with great surprise, that as he looked, he saw this bell begin to swing. It rang out loudly, and so did every bell in the house.

This might have lasted a minute, but it seemed an hour. The bells stopped only to be replaced by a clanking noise, as if someone were dragging a heavy chain. Scrooge had heard that ghosts in haunted houses were described as dragging chains.

"It's humbug still!" said Scrooge.

His color changed though, when without a pause, it came on through the heavy door, and passed into the room before his eyes. Upon its coming in, the dying flame leaped up as though it cried, "I know him! Marley's Ghost!" and fell again.

The same face: the very same. Marley in his pigtail, usual waistcoat, tights, and boots. The chain he drew was clasped about his waist. It was long, and wound about his ghostly form like a tail. It was made of cash-

boxes, keys, padlocks, ledgers, deeds, and heavy steel purses.

"How now!" said Scrooge, "who are you?"

"In life I was your partner, Jacob Marley. You don't believe in me," observed the Ghost.

"I don't," said Scrooge.

"Why do you doubt your senses?"

"Because," said Scrooge, "a little thing affects them. A slight disorder of the stomach makes one's senses cheat. You may be an undigested bit of beef, a blot of mustard, a crumb of cheese, a fragment of an underdone potato. There's more of gravy about you than of the grave."

At this the spirit raised a frightful cry, and shook its chain with such a dismal and frightening noise, that Scrooge fell upon his knees and clasped his hands before his face.

"Mercy!" he said. "Dreadful spirit, I do believe in you. I must. But why do you trouble me?"

"It is required of every man," the Ghost returned, "that the spirit within him should walk among his fellow-men, and travel far and wide; and if that spirit goes not forth in life, it is condemned to do so after death. It is doomed to wander through the world — oh, woe is me! — and witness what it cannot share, but might have shared on earth, and turned to happiness!"

"Why are you chained?" asked Scrooge.

"I wear the chain I forged in life," replied the Ghost. "I made it link by link, and yard by yard; and of my own free will I wore it. Is it strange to *you*? Or would you know the weight and length of the strong coil you bear yourself? It was full as heavy and as long as this, seven

Christmas Eves ago. You have labored on it, since. It is a ponderous chain!"

"Jacob," Scrooge begged. "Old Jacob Marley, tell me more. Speak comfort to me, Jacob."

"I have none to give," the Ghost replied. "I cannot rest, I cannot stay, I cannot linger anywhere. In life my spirit never left the narrow limits of our money-changing hole. Weary journeys lie before me to make amends for wasting the chance to help others. Such was I! Oh! such was I!"

"But you were always a good man of business, Jacob," faltered Scrooge.

"Business!" cried the Ghost, wringing his hands again. "Mankind was my business. The common welfare, charity, mercy, were all my business. Hear me! My time is nearly gone. I am here to warn you that you have yet a chance of escaping what's happened to me. You will be haunted by Three Spirits. Without their visits, you cannot hope to avoid the path I walk. Expect the first tomorrow, when the bell tolls one; the second on the next night at the same hour; and the third, the next night on the last stroke of twelve."

Scrooge raised his eyes again, and found his visitor with its chain wound about its arm. The spirit walked backward, towards the slowly opening window. It beckoned Scrooge to approach. When they were within two paces of each other, Scrooge heard sorrowful noises in the air. The spirit floated out upon the night.

Scrooge looked out. The air was filled with phantoms, wandering in restless haste and moaning. Every one of them wore chains like Marley's Ghost; some few were linked together; none were free.

As he closed the window, Scrooge tried to say "Humbug!" but stopped. Exhausted, he went to bed without undressing, and fell asleep instantly.

When he awoke, it was so dark that he could scarcely distinguish the transparent window from the walls of his chamber. He was trying to pierce the darkness with his ferret eyes, when a neighboring church chimed the hour of twelve. He remembered that the Ghost had warned him of a visitation when the bell tolled one. He decided to lie awake until the hour was passed, and at long last the bell tolled.

Light flashed up in the room. The curtains of his bed were drawn aside and Scrooge faced another unearthly visitor. It was a strange, child-like figure, yet not so like a child as like an old man small as a child. Its hair, which hung about its neck and down its back, was white as if with age, and yet the face had not a wrinkle on it. The arms were very long and muscular; its legs and feet were bare. It wore a tunic of the purest white and round its waist was bound a gleaming belt. It held a branch of fresh green holly in its hand, yet had its dress trimmed with summer flowers. But the strangest thing about it was, that from the crown of its head there sprung a bright clear jet of light.

"Are you the Spirit, sir, whose coming was foretold to me?" asked Scrooge.

"I am." The voice was soft and gentle. "I am the Ghost of Christmas Past."

"Long past?" inquired Scrooge.

"No. Your past."

Scrooge then made bold to inquire what business brought him there.

"Your welfare!" said the Ghost. "Rise! and walk with me!"

It would not have helped for Scrooge to plead that the weather was poor and the hour late, and that he was only clad in his slippers, dressing-gown and nightcap. The grasp, though gentle as a woman's hand, was firm. He rose: but finding that the Spirit made towards the window, dragged behind.

"I will fall," Scrooge protested.

"Bear but a touch of my hand *there*," said the Spirit, laying it upon his heart, "and you shall be upheld in more than this!"

As the words were spoken, they passed through the wall, and stood upon an open country road, with fields on either hand. It was a clear, cold winter day, with snow upon the ground.

"Good Heaven!" said Scrooge, clasping his hands together. "I was a boy here!"

"Your lip is trembling," said the Ghost. "And what is that upon your cheek!"

Scrooge muttered, with an unusual catching in his voice, that it was only a pimple.

"Do you remember the way?" inquired the Spirit.

"Remember it?" cried Scrooge, "I could walk it blindfolded!"

They walked along the road until a little market-town appeared in the distance, with its bridge, its church and winding river. Boys upon shaggy ponies trotted towards them, shouting to each other, filling the fields with merry music.

"These are shadows of things that have been," said the Ghost. "They have no consciousness of us."

The travellers came on; and as they came, Scrooge knew and named every one. Why was he filled with gladness to see them; to hear them give each other Merry Christmas, as they headed for their homes? What was Merry Christmas to Scrooge? What good had it ever done him?

"The school is not quite deserted," said the Ghost. "A solitary child is left there still."

Scrooge said he knew it. And he sobbed. They soon approached a mansion of dull red brick, poorly furnished, cold, and vast. They went through a door into a long, bare room, made barer still by lines of plain desks. At one of these, a lonely boy was reading near a feeble fire; and Scrooge sat down, and wept to see his poor forgotten self as he used to be.

"I wish," Scrooge muttered, drying his eyes with his cuff: "but it's too late now."

"What is the matter?" asked the Spirit.

"Nothing," said Scrooge, "nothing. There was a boy singing at my door last night. I should like to have given him something, that's all."

Scrooge's former self grew larger and the room became a little darker and more dirty. There he was, alone again, when all the other boys had gone home for the holidays. He was not reading now, but walking up and down sadly. Scrooge glanced anxiously towards the door.

It opened; and a little girl, much younger than the boy, came darting in, and putting her arms about his neck, and often kissing him, addressed him as her "Dear, dear brother."

"I have come to bring you home!" said the child,

clapping her tiny hands, and bending down to laugh. "Home, forever and ever. Father is so much kinder than he used to be. You will never have to come back here, but first, we're to be together all the Christmas long!"

"You are quite a woman, little Fan!" exclaimed the boy.

"Always a delicate creature," said the Ghost. "But she had a large heart! She died a woman and had, as I think, children."

"One child," Scrooge said, uneasily, "my nephew."

They left the school behind them, and were now in a busy city. The Ghost stopped at a certain warehouse door.

"I trained there!" said Scrooge.

They went in. At the sight of an old gentleman sitting behind a high desk, Scrooge cried out:

"Why, it's old Fezziwig! Bless his heart!"

Old Fezziwig laid down his pen, and looked up at the clock, which pointed to the hour of seven.

"Yo ho, there! Ebenezer! Dick!"

Scrooge's former self, now a young man, came briskly in, accompanied by his fellow workers.

"Yo ho, my boys!" said Fezziwig. "No more work tonight. Christmas Eve, lads. Clear away, boys, and let's have lots of room here!"

It was done in a minute. Every movable was packed off, the floor was swept, fuel was heaped upon the fire; and the warehouse was as bright a ballroom as you would desire to see.

In came a fiddler with a music book. In came Mrs. Fezziwig, the three Miss Fezziwigs with their many suitors, and all the young men and women employed in the business. In they all came, one after another. Away they all went, twenty couples at once, round and round until old Fezziwig, clapping his hands to stop the dance, cried out, "Well done!" There were more dances and plenty of food and drink. Old Fezziwig danced with Mrs. Fezziwig. Hold hands with your partner, bow and curtsey, cork-screw, thread-the-needle, and back to your place! Fezziwig danced so deftly, that he appeared to wink with his legs.

During the whole of this time, Scrooge had acted like a man out of his wits. He remembered everything and enjoyed everything.

"A small matter," said the Ghost, "to make these silly folks so full of gratitude. He has spent but a few pounds of your mortal money."

"It isn't that, Spirit," said Scrooge. "He has the power to render us happy or unhappy; to make our service a pleasure or a toil. The happiness he gives is quite as great as if it cost a fortune" — he felt the Spirit's glance, and stopped.

"What is the matter?" asked the Ghost.

"Nothing," said Scrooge. "I should like to say a word or two to my clerk just now! That's all."

"My time grows short," observed the Spirit.

This was not addressed to Scrooge, but it produced an immediate effect, for again Scrooge saw himself. He was older now; a man in the prime of his life. His face had begun to wear the signs of care and greed.

He was not alone, but sat by the side of a fair young girl in whose eyes there were tears.

"Another idol has displaced me," she said, softly, "a

golden one; and if it can cheer and comfort you in time to come, I have no just cause to grieve."

"This is the way of the world!" he said. "There is nothing on which it is so hard as poverty; and there is nothing it condemns with such severity as the pursuit of wealth!"

"Our contract is an old one," continued the girl. "It was made when we were both poor and content to be so. When it was made, you were another man. How often and how keenly I have thought of this, I will not say. It is enough that I *have* thought of it, and can release you."

"Have I ever asked to be released?" asked Scrooge, impatiently.

"In words? No. Never. But you have changed. If you were free today, would you choose a poor girl; you who weigh everything by gain? And if you did, I know regret would surely follow. And so, I release you. May you be happy in the life you have chosen." She left him and they parted.

"Spirit!" said Scrooge, "show me no more! Why do you delight to torture me? Remove me from this place!"

"I told you these were shadows of the things that have been," said the Ghost. "That they are what they are, do not blame me!"

"Leave me! Take me back! Haunt me no longer!"

He was conscious of being exhausted, and aware of being back in his own bedroom. He was overcome by sleepiness and he barely had time to reel into bed, before he sank into a heavy sleep.

Awaking in the middle of a very tough snore, Scrooge sat up in bed to gather his thoughts. He felt that he was restored to consciousness for the purpose of meeting the second Spirit. The Bell struck One, and no shape appeared. A quarter of an hour went by, yet nothing came. But, all this time a blaze of ruddy light had streamed upon his bed since the clock told the hour. He began to think that the source and secret of this ghostly light might be in the next room. He got up softly and shuffled in his slippers to the door.

A strange voice called him by name, and ordered him to enter. He obeyed.

It was his own room, but it had undergone a surprising change. The walls and ceiling were so hung with holly, that the room looked like a grove. Heaped up on the floor, to form a kind of throne, were turkeys, geese, game, great joints of meat, plum puddings, fruits of every description, and steaming bowls of punch. Upon this couch there sat a jolly Giant, glorious to see. He held a glowing torch in shape not unlike Plenty's horn, and held it up to shed its light on Scrooge as he came peeping round the door.

"I am the Ghost of Christmas Present," said the Spirit. "Come in and know me better. Look upon me! You have never seen the like of me before!"

Scrooge looked closely at the Spirit. It was clothed in one simple deep green robe, or mantle, bordered with white fur. On its head it wore a holly wreath, set here and there with shining icicles. Its dark brown curls were long and free — free as its jolly face, its sparkling eye, its cheery voice, and its joyful air.

The Ghost of Christmas Present rose.

"Spirit," said Scrooge almost bowing, "bring me where you will. I went forth last night and I learned a

lesson which is working now. Tonight, if you have something to teach me, let me profit by it."

"Touch my robe!"

Scrooge did as he was told, and held fast.

The room vanished instantly and Scrooge found himself standing in the city streets on Christmas morning. The house fronts were black and the windows blacker, in contrast with the smooth white snow. They went on, invisible, into the suburbs of the town, straight to Scrooge's clerk's home. On the threshold of the door, the Spirit stopped to bless Bob Cratchit's dwelling with a sprinkling of his torch.

Once inside, they watched Mrs. Cratchit and daughter Belinda set the table, while young Peter Cratchit plunged a fork into a saucepan of potatoes. And now two smaller Cratchits, boy and girl, came tearing in and danced around the table.

"What has ever got your precious father, then?" said Mrs. Cratchit. "And your brother, Tiny Tim; and where is our Martha?"

"Here's Martha, mother!" said a girl, appearing as she spoke.

"Why bless your heart, dear, how late you are!"

"Father is coming," cried the two young Cratchits. "Hide, Martha, hide!"

So Martha hid herself, and in came Bob Cratchit in his threadbare clothes and Tiny Tim on his shoulder. Tiny Tim held a crutch and his limbs were supported by an iron frame.

"Why, where's our Martha?" cried Bob Cratchit.

"Not coming," said Mrs. Cratchit.

Martha didn't like to see him disappointed, so she

came out from behind the closet door, and ran into his arms, while the two young Cratchits bore Tiny Tim off to the washhouse.

"And how did Tiny Tim behave?" asked Mrs. Cratchit.

"As good as gold," said Bob, "and better. Somehow he gets thoughtful sitting by himself so much. He told me that he hoped the people saw him in church, because he was a cripple, and it might be pleasant to them to remember upon Christmas Day who made lame beggars walk."

A crutch was heard upon the floor, and back came Tiny Tim, escorted by his brother and sister. Bob began putting together a hot mixture in a jug with gin and lemons and hung it in the fireplace to simmer. Peter and the two younger Cratchits went to fetch the goose, with which they soon returned.

There never was such a goose. Bob said he didn't believe there ever was such a goose cooked. Its tenderness and flavor, size and cheapness, were all admired by everyone. With applesauce and mashed potatoes added, it was sufficient dinner for the whole family.

But now, the plates being changed by Belinda, Mrs. Cratchit left the room to take the pudding up, and bring it in. In half a minute Mrs. Cratchit entered, smiling proudly, with the pudding blazing in a pint of fiery brandy.

At last the dinner was all done, the cloth cleared and the fire made up. The compound in the jug, being tasted and considered perfect, was served to everyone. Then all the Cratchit family drew round the hearth.

"A Merry Christmas to us all, my dears. God bless us!" Bob said.

Which all the family re-echoed.

"God bless us every one!" said Tiny Tim.

He sat very close to his father's side, upon his little stool. Bob held Tiny Tim's withered little hand in his.

"Spirit," said Scrooge, with an interest he had never felt before, "tell me if Tiny Tim will live."

"I see a vacant seat," replied the Ghost, "and a crutch without an owner, carefully preserved. If these shadows remain unchanged by the Future, the child will die."

"Oh no, kind Spirit," said Scrooge. "Say he will be spared."

"If these shadows remain unchanged by the Future," replied the Ghost, "next Christmas will not find him here. What then? If he be like to die, he had better do it, and decrease the extra population."

Scrooge hung his head to hear his own words quoted, and was overcome with grief. He cast his eyes on the ground, but raised them speedily on hearing his name.

"I give you Mr. Scrooge!" said Bob. "The Founder of the Feast!"

"The Founder of the Feast, indeed!" cried Mrs. Cratchit. "I wish I had him here. I'd give him a piece of my mind to feast upon."

"My dear," said Bob, "it's Christmas Day."

"I'll drink to his health for your sake and the day's," said Mrs. Cratchit, "not for his. Long life to him! A Merry Christmas and a Happy New Year!"

The children drank the toast after her, but the men-

tion of Scrooge's name cast a dark shadow on the party, which did not leave for a full five minutes.

After it had passed away, they were ten times merrier than before and told tales and sang songs. They were not a handsome family; they were not well dressed; their shoes were far from waterproof; their clothes were scanty: and yet they were happy, grateful, and pleased with one another and contented with the time. Scrooge watched them, and especially Tiny Tim.

By this time, it was getting dark and snowing pretty heavily. As Scrooge and the Spirit went along the streets, the brightness of the roaring fires in kitchens, parlors, and other rooms was wonderful. How the Ghost beamed! How it spread, with generous hand, its bright and harmless joy on everything within its reach!

And now, without a word of warning from the Ghost, they stood upon a bleak and deserted spot.

"This is a place where Miners live," said the Spirit. "But they know me. See!"

A light shone from the window of a hut, and they advanced towards it. Inside they found a cheerful company assembled around a glowing fire. An old man and woman, together with their entire family, sat decked out in holiday attire and sang a Christmas song.

The Spirit did not delay here, but bade Scrooge hold his robe, and passing on above the land, sped across the sea. To Scrooge's horror, looking back, he saw the last of the land behind them.

Built upon a dismal reef of sunken rocks, there stood a solitary lighthouse. But even here, two men who watched the light had made a fire and joining hands over the table at which they sat, wished each other a Merry

Christmas. One of them, the elder one, struck up a sturdy song.

Again the Ghost sped on, above the black and heaving sea until they lighted on a ship. Every man among them hummed a Christmas tune, or had a Christmas thought, or spoke to his friend of some past Christmas Day. Scrooge was deep in thought as they moved through the darkness, listening to the moaning wind.

It was a great surprise to Scrooge to hear a hearty laugh. It was an even greater surprise to Scrooge to recognize the laugh as his own nephew's. He found himself in a bright room, with the Spirit standing by his side and looking at that same nephew with an approving smile.

"Ha, ha!" laughed Fred. "Ha, ha, ha!"

When Fred laughed in this way — holding his sides and twisting his head — Scrooge's niece by marriage laughed as heartily as he. And their friends also roared out, happily.

"He said that Christmas was a humbug!" cried Scrooge's nephew. "And he believed it, too!"

"More shame for him, Fred!" declared Scrooge's niece.

"He's a comical old fellow," said his nephew, "that's the truth: and not so pleasant as he might be. However, his offenses bring on their own punishment, and I have nothing to say against him."

"I'm sure he's very rich," hinted his niece.

"Yes, but his wealth is of no use to him. He doesn't do any good with it and he doesn't make himself comfortable with it. I'm sorry for him; I couldn't be angry with him if I tried. Who suffers by his ill whims? Only him! If he won't come and dine with us, what's the result! He just loses a very good dinner."

Scrooge's nephew revelled in another laugh, and soon everyone caught his laughter and followed his example.

"I was going to say," continued Scrooge's nephew, "that the consequence of his not making merry with us, is that he loses some pleasant memories. I mean to give him the same chance every year, whether he likes it or not, for I pity him."

After tea they had some music, for they were a musical family. Scrooge's niece played upon the harp a song from Scrooge's childhood. When this strain of music sounded, all the things the Ghosts had shown Scrooge came upon his mind, and he thought that if he could have listened to it often, years ago, he might have developed the kindnesses of life for his own happiness.

But the party didn't devote the whole evening to music. After awhile they played at blindman's bluff. There were more games. When they played the game "How, When, and Where," even old Scrooge joined in, despite the fact that he couldn't be seen. In fact, Uncle Scrooge had imperceptibly become so gay and light of heart, that he begged like a boy to be allowed to stay until the guests had departed. The Ghost was pleased to find him in this mood, but said that this could not be done.

The whole scene passed away and they were off, once again, on their travels. Much they saw, and far they went, and many homes they visited, but always with a happy end. Wherever they went, the Spirit left his blessing and taught Scrooge a lesson.

It was a long night, if it were only a night. Scrooge had his doubts, because the Christmas holidays appeared to be condensed in time as they passed. It was strange, too, that the Spirit had grown older, its hair graying.

"Are spirits' lives so short?" asked Scrooge, as they stood in an open place.

"My life upon this globe is very brief," replied the Ghost. "It ends tonight at midnight. Hark! The time is drawing near."

The chimes were ringing three quarters past eleven at that moment. "Forgive me," said Scrooge, "but I see something strange under your robe. Is it a foot or a claw?"

"Oh Man! look here. Look down here!" exclaimed the Ghost, as he brought out two children; ragged, scowling, wolfish, ugly, but humble, too. Where graceful youth should have filled their features out and touched them with fresh tints, a stale hand, like that of age, had pinched and twisted them and pulled them to shreds. Where angels might have sat, devils lurked and glared out.

Scrooge started back. He tried to say they were fine children, but the words choked themselves, rather than be parties to such an enormous lie.

"Spirit! are they yours?" Scrooge asked, horrified. He could say no more.

"They are Man's," said the Spirit, "and they cling to me, appealing from their fathers. This boy is Ignorance. This girl is Want. Beware them both, but most of all beware the boy, for on his brow I see that written which is Doom, unless the writing be erased."

"Have they no refuge or resource?" cried Scrooge.

"Are there no prisons?" said the Spirit, turning on him for the last time his own words. "Are there no workhouses?"

The bell struck twelve.

Scrooge looked about him for the Ghost, and saw it not. As the last stroke ceased to vibrate, he remembered the prediction of Jacob Marley, and lifting up his eyes, beheld a solemn Phantom, draped and hooded, coming like a mist along the ground towards him.

The Phantom slowly, gravely, silently, approached. Scrooge bent down upon his knee; for the Spirit seemed to scatter gloom and mystery in the very air through which it moved.

It was wearing a deep black garment, which concealed its face and form, and left nothing of it visible save one outstretched hand. Even this hand would have been difficult to detach from the darkness which surrounded the Phantom. Although he felt it tall and stately, its mysterious presence filled him with a solemn dread. He knew no more, for the Spirit neither spoke nor moved.

"Am I in the presence of the Ghost of Christmas Yet to Come?" said Scrooge.

The Spirit answered not, but pointed onward with its hand.

"You are about to show me shadows of the things that have not happened, but will happen in the time before us?" Scrooge pursued. "Is that so, Spirit?"

The upper portion of the garment was contracted for an instant in its folds, as if the Spirit had inclined its head. That was the only answer he received.

Though accustomed to ghostly company by now,

Scrooge's legs trembled beneath him, and he found that he could hardly start to prepare to follow it. The Spirit paused a moment, watching his condition, and gave him time to recover.

But Scrooge was all the worse for this. It thrilled him with vague, uncertain horror to know that behind the dark hood were ghostly eyes intently fixed on him, while he, though stretching his own to the utmost, could see nothing but a ghostly hand and one great heap of black.

"Ghost of the Future!" he exclaimed, "I fear you more than any spirit I have seen. But as I know your purpose is to do me good, and as I hope to live to be another man from what I was, I am prepared to bear your company, and do it with a thankful heart. Will you not speak to me?"

It gave no reply. The hand was pointed straight before them.

"Lead on! The night is waning fast, and it is precious time to me," Scrooge said. "Lead on!"

The Phantom moved away as it had come towards him. Scrooge followed in the shadow of its dress, which bore him up and carried him along.

They scarcely seemed to enter the city. Rather the city seemed to spring up about them and surround them. There they were in the heart of it. Scrooge found himself among the merchants and businessmen who hurried up and down and clinked money in their pockets. They talked in small groups and looked at their watches and toyed thoughtfully with their great gold seals, and so forth as Scrooge had often seen them.

The Spirit stopped beside a group of businessmen.

Observing that the hand was pointed to them, Scrooge advanced to listen to their talk.

"No," said a great fat man with a monstrous chin, "I don't know much about it. I only know he is dead."

"When did he die?" inquired another.

"Last night, I believe."

"Why, what was the matter with him?" asked a third, taking a vast quantity of snuff out of a very large snuff-box. "I thought he would never die."

"God knows," said the first, with a yawn.

"What has he done with his money?" asked a red-faced gentleman, with a drooping growth at the end of his nose, that shook like the gills of a turkey cock.

"I haven't heard," said the man with the large chin, yawning again. "Left it to his Company, perhaps. I only know he hasn't left it to *me*."

This joke was received with a laugh.

"It's likely to be a very cheap funeral," said the same speaker. "I don't know anybody who would go to it. I don't mind going if a lunch is provided, but I must be fed."

Another laugh.

Speakers and listeners walked away, mixing with other groups. The Phantom glided on into the street. Its finger pointed to two persons meeting.

"How are you?" said one.

"How are you?" said the other.

"Well!" said the first, "the Devil has got his own at last, hey?"

"So I am told," returned the second. "Cold, isn't it? You're not a skater, I suppose?"

"No, no. Good morning."

Scrooge was at first surprised that the Spirit should attach importance to conversations so trivial; but feeling assured that they must have some hidden purpose, he considered what it was. He could not think of anyone immediately connected with himself, to whom he could apply them. He looked about for himself, but another man stood in his accustomed corner. It gave him little surprise, however, for he had been thinking of making changes in his life, and thought and hoped he saw his newborn resolutions carried out in this.

They left the busy scene, and went into an obscure and bad part of town. The ways were foul and narrow; the shops and houses wretched; the people half-naked, drunken and ugly. The whole quarter reeked of crime, filth and misery.

Far in this wicked den, there was a shop where iron, old rags, bottles and bones were brought. Sitting among the wares he dealt in was a gray-haired rascal who smoked his pipe peacefully.

Just then a cleaning woman with a heavy bundle slunk into the shop. She had scarcely entered, when another woman with a bundle, a laundress, came in, too. She was closely followed by the undertaker, who was no less startled by the sight of them, than they had been upon seeing each other. After a short period of blank astonishment, they all burst out laughing.

"You couldn't have met at a better place," said old Joe, removing his pipe from his mouth. "Come into the parlor."

The parlor was a space behind a screen of rags. The old man raked the fire together with an old stair-rod and relit his pipe. Meanwhile, the cleaning woman threw her bundle on the floor and gave the other two a look of cold defiance.

"What's the problem?" said the woman. "Every person has the right to take care of themselves. *He* always did!"

"That's true, indeed!" said the laundress, Mrs. Dilber. "No man more so."

"Very well, then!" cried the cleaning woman, "Who's the worse for the loss of a few things like these? Not a dead man! If he wanted to keep them after, why wasn't he natural in his lifetime? If he had been, he'd have had somebody to look after him when he was dying, instead of gasping out his last breath there, alone. Open that bundle, old Joe, and let me know the value of it!"

The undertaker, however, produced his stolen goods first. A pencil-case, a pair of sleeve-buttons, and a scarf pin of no great value were all appraised by old Joe, who added the sums he would give for each, upon the wall.

Mrs. Dilber was next. She had sheets and towels, a little wearing apparel, two silver teaspoons, and a few boots. Her account was also written on the wall.

"I always give too much to the ladies," said old Joe. "It's a weakness of mine."

Joe then went down on his knees to examine the cleaning woman's bundle. After unfastening a great many knots, she dragged out a set of curtains.

"You don't mean to say you took 'em down, rings and all, with him lying there?" asked Joe.

"Yes, I do," replied the woman. "Why not?"

"You were born to make a fortune," said Joe.

Scrooge listened to this dialogue in horror. He viewed them with disgust as they sat around their loot; his hatred of them could hardly have been greater, had they been obscene demons selling the corpse itself.

"Ha, ha!" laughed the cleaning woman, when old Joe produced the bag of money. "This is the end of it, you see! He frightened everyone away when he was alive, to profit us when he was dead!"

"Spirit!" said Scrooge, shuddering from head to foot. "I see, I see. The case of this unhappy man might be my own. My life tends that way, now — merciful Heaven, what is this!"

He drew back in terror, for the scene had changed. He now stood near a bare, uncurtained bed, on which, beneath a ragged sheet, there lay a something covered up.

The room was very dark, yet a pale light, rising in the outer air, fell straight upon the bed and on the body of a man.

Scrooge glanced towards the Phantom. Its steady hand was pointed to the head. The slightest raising of the cover would have disclosed the face. He longed to do it, but had no more power to withdraw the veil than to dismiss the spectre at his side.

This man lay in a dark empty house, with no one to say a kind word. Scrooge thought that if this man could be raised up now, what would be his foremost thoughts? Greed, hard dealing, griping cares? They have brought him to a rich end, truly!

He turned to the Spirit. "This is a fearful place. In leaving it, I shall not leave its lesson, trust me. Let us go!"

Still the Ghost pointed with an unmoved finger to the head.

"I understand you," Scrooge returned, "but I have not the power to do it, Spirit."

Again it seemed to look upon him.

"Show me some tenderness with death," said Scrooge, "or this dark chamber will be all I remember."

The Ghost led him through several familiar streets. As they went along, Scrooge looked here and there to find himself, but nowhere was he to be seen. They entered Bob Cratchit's house, and found the mother and the children seated around the fire.

The usually noisy little Cratchits were as still as statues in one corner, looking at Peter, who was reading. The mother and her daughters were sewing. They, too, were very quiet!

The mother laid her work upon the table, and put her hand up to her face. "The color hurts my eyes," she said.

The color? Ah, poor Tiny Tim!

"They're better now again," said Cratchit's wife. "It makes them weak by candlelight; and I wouldn't show weak eyes to your father when he comes home, for the world. It must be near his time."

"Past it, rather," Peter answered. "But I think he's walked a little slower than he used to, these last few evenings, mother."

"I have known him to walk very fast with — with Tiny Tim upon his shoulders."

"And so have I!" they all exclaimed.

"His father loved him so, that he was light to carry," she resumed. "Here is your father, now!"

She hurried to meet her husband. As he sat down, the two young Cratchits got upon his knees and kissing him, said, "Don't be grieved, Father."

"You went today then, Robert?" said his wife.

"Yes, my dear," returned Bob. "I wish you could have seen how green it is. I promised him that I would walk there on Sunday. My little, little child!"

He broke down all at once. He couldn't help it. If he could have helped it, he and his child would have been farther apart than they were.

They drew together and talked. Bob told them of the kindness of Mr. Scrooge's nephew. "Upon hearing of the tragedy, Fred said, 'I am heartily sorry for it, Mr. Cratchit, and sorry for your good wife. If I can be of any service to you, here is my address.' It really seemed as if he had known our Tiny Tim, and felt with us."

"I'm sure he is a good soul!" said Mrs. Cratchit.

"I wouldn't be surprised," returned Bob, "if he got Peter a better situation."

"Get along with you!" said Peter, grinning.

"It's just as likely as not," said Bob. "But whenever we part from one another, we shall not forget Tiny Tim, shall we?"

"Never, father!" they all cried.

"And I know," said Bob, "that when we recall how patient he was, we shall not quarrel easily among ourselves."

"No, never, father!" they all cried again.

"I am very happy," said Bob, "very happy!"

Then Mrs. Cratchit, his daughters, and the two young Cratchits kissed him; Peter and he shook hands.

"Spectre," said Scrooge, "something informs me that

our parting is at hand. Tell me what man that was whom we saw lying dead?"

The Ghost conveyed him to a familiar part of the city. "This court," said Scrooge, "is where my counting-house is. Let me behold what I shall be in days to come."

He hastened to the window of his office. The furniture was not the same, and the figure in the chair was not himself. The Spirit pointed in another direction.

Scrooge paused before entering the iron gate to a churchyard. Walled in by houses, the yard was overrun by weeds, the growth of death, not life; fat with repleted appetite of too much burying. Here lay buried, the wretched man whose name he had now to learn.

The Spirit stood among the graves, and pointed down to One. Scrooge advanced towards it trembling.

"Before I draw nearer to that stone, answer me one question," said Scrooge. "Are these the shadows of the things that Will be, or are they shadows of things that only May be?"

Still the Ghost pointed downward to the grave.

"Men's courses may lead to certain ends," said Scrooge. "But if the courses change, so will the ends. Say it is thus with what you show me!"

The Spirit spoke not a word.

Scrooge crept towards the grave, trembling. Following the finger, he read upon the stone of the neglected grave his own name, EBENEZER SCROOGE.

"Am *I* that man who lay upon the bed?" he cried, upon his knees.

The finger pointed from the grave to him, and back again.

"No, Spirit!" he cried, clutching at its robe, "hear

EBENEZER
SCROOGE

me! I am not the man I was. Why show me this, if I am past all hope?"

For the first time, the Phantom's hand appeared to shake.

"I will honor Christmas in my heart all the year. I will live in the Past, Present, and the Future. I will not shut out the lessons that they teach. Oh, tell me I may sponge away the writing on this stone!"

In his agony, he caught the ghostly hand. It sought to free itself, but he was strong and detained it. The Spirit, stronger yet, repulsed him.

While making a last prayer, he saw the Phantom's hood and dress shrink, collapse and dwindle down into a bedpost. Yes! the bedpost — the room — were his own! Happiest of all, he had Time before him to make changes!

"I will live with the Spirits of the Past, the Present, and the Future in me!" Scrooge repeated, as he scrambled out of bed. "Heaven and the Christmas Time be praised! I say it on my knees, Jacob Marley!"

He was so fluttered in his good intentions, that his voice broke. He had been sobbing violently in his conflict with the Spirit, and his face was wet with tears.

Scrooge folded one of his bed-curtains in his arms. "They are not torn down; they are here. I am here! The shadows of things that would have been, will be dispelled! I don't know what to do!" cried Scrooge, laughing and crying at once. "I was as light as a feather — as merry as a schoolboy. A Merry Christmas to everybody! A Happy New Year to all the world! Whoop! Hallo!"

He had skipped into the sitting-room and now stood perfectly winded. "There is the door, by which the Ghost of Jacob Marley entered!" cried Scrooge. "There's the corner where the Ghost of Christmas Present sat! It's all true, it all happened. Ha, ha, ha!"

"I don't know what day it is!" said Scrooge. "I don't know how long I've been with the Spirits."

Suddenly, there was the clash, clang, ding, dong of church bells ringing everywhere. Scrooge opened the window and put his head out. No fog, no mist; clear, bright cold, making blood dance. Golden sunlight, heavenly sky and fresh air with the ringing of merry bells.

"What's today?" cried Scrooge, calling to a boy in Sunday clothes.

"Today? Why CHRISTMAS DAY!" replied the boy.

"It's Christmas Day! I haven't missed it," said Scrooge. "Hallo, do you know the Poulterer's?"

"I should hope I did," replied the lad.

"An intelligent, remarkable boy!" said Scrooge. "Do you know whether they've sold their prize turkey? Not the little one, the big one?"

"What, the one as big as me? It's hanging there now," replied the boy.

"What a delightful boy!" said Scrooge. "Go and buy it."

"Walk-ER!" exclaimed the boy.

"I am in earnest," said Scrooge. "Tell'em to bring it here. Come back with the man, and I'll give you a shilling. Be back in less than five minutes, and I'll give you half-a-crown!"

The boy was off like a shot.

"I'll send it to Bob Cratchit's!" whispered Scrooge, rubbing his hands. "He shan't know who sends it. It's twice the size of Tiny Tim."

He wrote the address in an unsteady hand and went downstairs to open the door. As he did, the knocker caught his eye.

"I shall love it as long as I live!" cried Scrooge, patting it with his hand. "What an honest expression it has! It's a wonderful knocker! —Here's the turkey. Hallo! How are you? Merry Christmas! Why, it's impossible to carry that to Camden Town; you must have a cab."

He chuckled as he paid for the turkey and the cab. Then he chuckled as he paid the boy half-a-crown. He was still chuckling as he sat down breathless in his chair again.

Shaving was not an easy task, for his hand shook. At last he was dressed and in the street. People were pouring forth as he had seen them with the Ghost of Christmas Present. Walking with his hands behind him, Scrooge looked so irresistibly pleasant, in a word, that three or four good-humored fellows said, "Good morning, sir! A Merry Christmas to you!" And Scrooge said often afterwards, that of all the happy sounds he had ever heard, those were the happiest in his ears.

Soon he beheld the portly gentleman who had walked into his counting-house the day before and it sent a pang across his heart. He knew what path lay straight before him, and he took it.

"My dear sir," said Scrooge, quickening his pace, and taking the old gentleman by both his hands. "How do you do? A Merry Christmas to you!"

"Mr. Scrooge?"

"I fear my name may not be pleasant to you. Al-

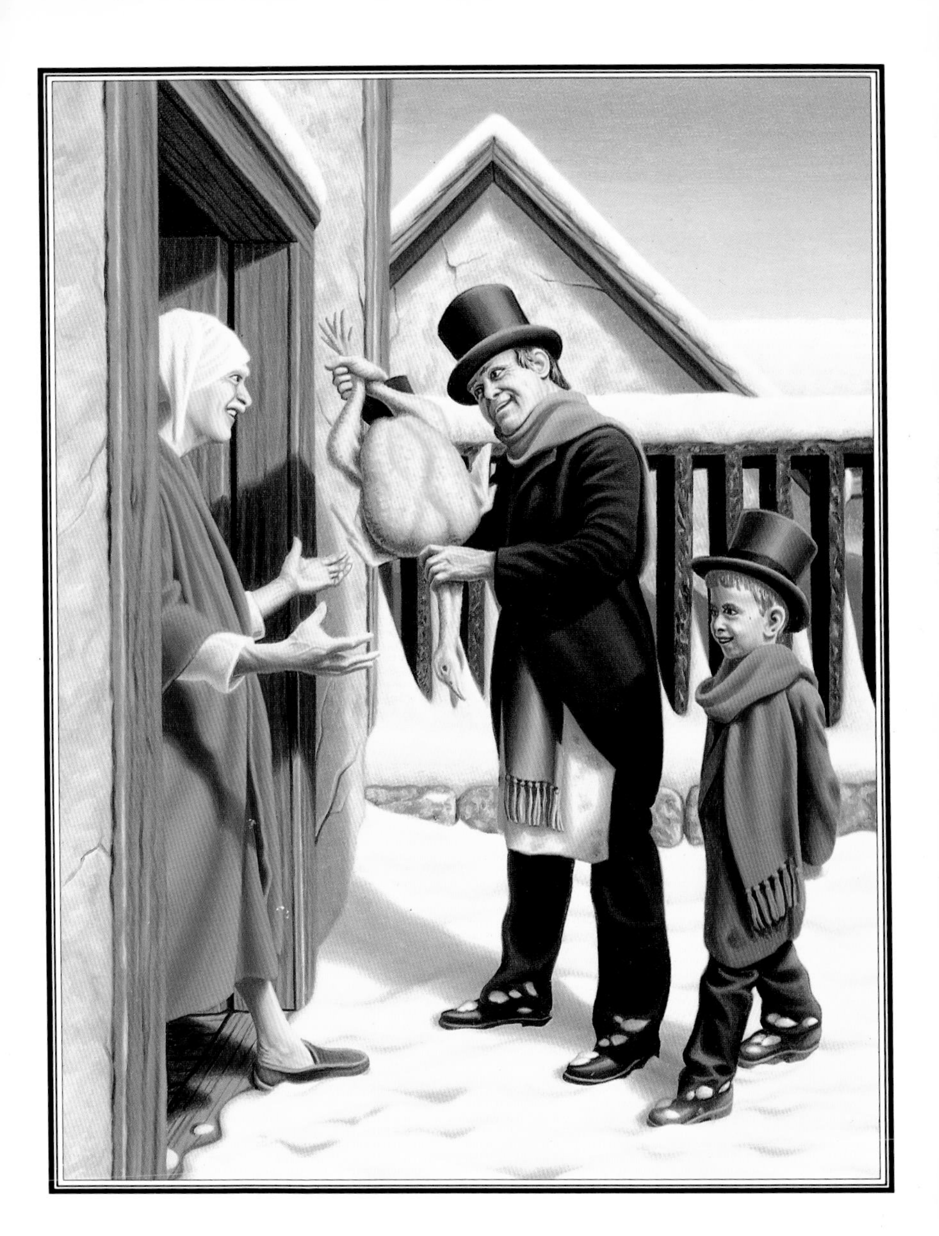

low me to ask your pardon. And will you have the goodness" — here Scrooge whispered in his ear.

"Lord bless me!" cried the gentleman. "My dear Mr. Scrooge, are you serious?"

"Not a farthing less," said Scrooge. "A great many back-payments are included in it!"

"My dear sir," said the other, shaking hands with him. "I don't know what to say —"

"Don't say anything, please," answered Scrooge. "Will you come and see me?"

"I will!" cried the old gentleman.

"Thank'ee," said Scrooge. "I am much obliged to you. I thank you fifty times. Bless you!"

He went to church, and walked about the streets, watching people hurrying to and fro. He patted children on the head and questioned beggars. He had never dreamed that anything could give him so much happiness. In the afternoon, he turned his steps towards his nephew's house.

He passed the door a dozen times, before he had the courage to knock. But he made a dash, and did it. "Is your master at home, my dear?" said Scrooge to the girl.

"Yes, sir. He's in the dining room with the mistress. I'll show you upstairs, if you please."

"He knows me," said Scrooge, with his hand already on the dining-room lock. "I'll go in here, my dear."

He turned it gently, and eased his face in, round the door. They were looking at the table, which was spread out in great array.

"Fred!" said Scrooge.

Dear heart alive, how his niece by marriage started! Scrooge had forgotten about her sitting in the corner with the footstool.

"Why bless my soul!" cried Fred, "who's that!"

"It's I. Your uncle Scrooge. I have come to dinner. Will you let me in, Fred?"

Let him in! It is a mercy he didn't shake his arm off. He was at home in five minutes. Nothing could be heartier. His niece looked just the same. So did everyone when *they* came. Wonderful party games, won-der-ful happiness!

He was early at the office next morning. He wanted to catch Bob Cratchit coming late! That was the thing he had set his heart upon.

And he did it; yes, he did! The clock struck nine. No Bob. A quarter past. No Bob. He was full eighteen minutes and a half behind his time. Scrooge sat with his door wide open.

Bob's hat was off before he opened the door. He was on his stool in a jiffy; driving away with his pen, as if he were trying to overtake nine o'clock.

"Hallo!" growled Scrooge, in his usual voice as nearly as he could make it. "What do you mean by coming here at this time of day?"

"I am very sorry, sir," said Bob.

"Yes, I think you are," said Scrooge. "Step this way, if you please."

"It's only once a year, sir," pleaded Bob. "It shall not be repeated. I was making rather merry yesterday, sir."

"Now, I'll tell you what, my friend," said Scrooge. "I am not going to stand this sort of thing any longer.

And therefore," he continued, leaping from his stool, "I am about to raise your salary!"

Bob trembled and had a momentary idea of knocking Scrooge down and calling to the people in the court for help and a straight-waistcoat.

"A Merry Christmas, Bob!" said Scrooge, as he clapped him on the back. "A merrier Christmas, Bob, my good fellow, than I have ever given you. I'll raise your salary and endeavor to assist your struggling family. Make up the fires before you dot another i, Bob Cratchit!"

Scrooge was better than his word. He did it all, and infinitely more; and to Tiny Tim, who did NOT die, he was a second father. He became as good a friend, as good a master, and as good a man, as the old city knew. Some people laughed to see the change in him, but he let them laugh. He was wise enough to know that nothing happens for good, but that some people laugh at the beginning.

He had no further conversations with Spirits, but lived upon the Total Abstinence Principle, ever afterwards; and it was always said of him that he knew how to keep Christmas well, if any man alive possessed the knowledge. May that be truly said of us, and all of us! And so, as Tiny Tim observed, God Bless Us, Every One!

THE END

ABOUT THE ILLUSTRATOR

Walt Sturrock was born in Jersey City, NJ in 1961. He became interested in art when he was very young. Eric Sloane and Maxfield Parrish were two of his favorite artists. After high school, he earned his degree in illustration from Montclair State College and began his career working in advertising, magazine, and book illustration. His work has also been shown in a number of galleries on the east coast. *A Christmas Carol* was Walt's first book for Unicorn Publishing, and his second book is *Aesop's Fables*. Walt is looking forward to continuing to illustrate more classics.